Alice Walker
BANNED

Alice Walker
BANNED

with an introduction by
Patricia Holt

aunt lute books
SAN FRANCISCO

Aunt Lute Books
P.O. Box 410687
San Francisco, CA 94141

10 9 8 7 6 5 4 3 2 1

Cover Photo: Jean Weisinger, "Woman With an Attitude"
Cover and Text Design: Pamela Wilson Design Studio
Typesetting: Pamela Wilson Design Studio
Senior Editor: Joan Pinkvoss
Book Editor: Shaleen Brawn

Research:	Production:	
Rachel Cleary	Lirio Adlawan	Tricia Lambie
JeeYeun Lee	Cristina Azócar	Norma Torres
Christine Scudder	Jonna K. Eagle	

Printed in the U.S.A. on acid-free paper.
This book was funded in part by grants from the National Endowment for
the Arts and the California Arts Council.

Library of Congress Cataloging-in-Publication Data

Walker, Alice, 1944-
   Alice Walker banned / with an introduction by Patricia Holt
     p. cm.
   ISBN 1-879960-47-8 (hc : alk. paper)
   1. Afro-Americans–Fiction. 2. Walker, Alice, 1944- –Censorship.
   3. Prohibited books–United States. I. Title.
   PS3573.A425A6 1996
   813'.54–dc20
                                96-18341
                                    CIP

Table of Contents

INTRODUCTION

By Patricia Holt

Along with her Pulitzer Prize and American Book Award, Alice Walker has the honor of being one of the most censored writers in American literature. Like Mark Twain, John Steinbeck, Madeleine L'Engle and J.D. Salinger, Walker has been the subject of so much controversy that too often the artistry of her work has been lost in the politics of the moment.

This short volume invites readers to view several of her most engaging works—the two short stories, "Am I Blue?" and "Roselily"; and the beginning of her novel, *The Color Purple*—as a small but key body of work in its own right, and to examine separately the bizarre configurations of censorship that have forced Walker to respond to political attack.

At least one case of censorship would have been considered hilarious if it hadn't been—like so many cases of outright banning—so tragic. In fact, we can begin our own investigation as a story with comic overtones.

A funny thing happened to Alice Walker on her way to winning yet another prestigious literary prize. In 1994, the state of California, through its Board of Education, abruptly removed two of

Walker's stories from a statewide test for 10th graders, stating that one story, "Am I Blue?" was "anti-meat-eating," and the other story, "Roselily," was "anti-religious." Then the state of California, through its governor, attempted to give Walker an award declaring her a "state treasure."

Wait a minute, said Alice Walker, probably feeling more like Alice in Wonderland than an internationally respected author: It doesn't make sense to ban a person's work and call that same person a "state treasure" at the same time.

Don't worry, said an announcement from the governor's office: This decision by the Board of Education "does not represent censorship, far from it." What *did* the decision represent then? Why, nothing having to do with the governor's award, said the director of the California Arts Council, which sponsored the prizes (other "state treasures" declared that year were film producer Steven Spielberg, actor Hal Holbrook and artist David Hockney). "This awards program raises scholarships for young artists to attend the California State Summer School for the Arts, and we view this as quite separate from other issues."

Well, those issues can't be disconnected, said novelist Maxine Hong Kingston, a past recipient of the award. "By banning a selection because certain words offend a minority of the population," she wrote in an angry letter to the acting state superintendent of schools, "the California Department of Education fails to recognize its real value: the pursuit of truth." Withdrawing permission for the state to use *her* work in any state tests, Kingston urged the Board to "reconsider its decision."

Meanwhile, Alice Walker wrote a simple letter stating that "under the circumstances . . . I cannot accept the Governor's Award." Joining her in support of that decision was the American Civil Liberties Union, which expressed its own concern that the Board's move "violates the most basic tenets of freedom of expression." And joining the ACLU in support of Walker were the National Association for the Advancement of Colored People, the California Association of Teachers of English, the Anti-Defamation League, the California Teachers Association, the California Writing Project, the San Francisco Foundation, the People for the American Way and other institutions and authors. Thousands of teachers signed a petition supporting Walker and "hundreds of thousands of people" she said later, "denounced the decision."

But whoa, said the Governor of California, Pete Wilson. "I oppose censorship of any kind," he wrote in a letter to Alice Walker, asking her to reconsider her decision and accept the award. "I have not endorsed the removal from tests of any of your writings." In fact he blamed "a staff member" for issuing the wrong announcement about the matter "in my absence, without my knowledge, and to make matters worse . . . based on misinformation . . ."

That's interesting, said Walker's supporters, since the staff member discussed the issue with the

3

governor after the Board's decision became public and published the statement *for* the governor, but let's not dwell on inconsistencies for now: If indeed the governor was on Alice's side and opposed this kind of censorship, wouldn't he tell the Board to put Walker's stories back in the statewide test for 10th graders?

Well, no and no: Wilson simply sent a letter to Board of Education President Marion McDowell and Acting School Superintendent William Dawson stating that "we must oppose censorship of any kind. It contradicts my personal beliefs and betrays the principles upon which our free society is built. Any hint of biased selection of materials or censorship in the development of a test is intolerable." That sounded pretty good, though it stopped short of telling the Board to *do* something about the immediate problem.

Walker remained unconvinced. "I sincerely appreciate [the governor's] request that I reconsider acceptance," she announced in a prepared statement. "A few weeks ago, I would have been honored. However, I love California and respect its children too much to accept becoming a 'state treasure' in a state whose educators consider my work a menace to the 10th grade."

You have to applaud her sense of humor. "A menace to the 10th grade" is hardly an accurate characterization of Alice Walker's role in life, and yet the term does seem to echo the Board of Education's fear of the effect of Walker's stories.

Board Chair McDowell said that "Am I Blue?" was withdrawn since it had the appearance (there's that naughty obfuscating vagueness again) of being offensive "because it might be viewed as advocating a particular nutritional lifestyle" (and there's the "anti-meat-eating" reference, you see) and "seemed to violate rural children's family occupations."

We could make a joke about all those animal-slaughtering families sending their fragile 10th graders in to take a test that made them burst into tears, but for now let's just notice the kind of words employed in the censorship process—"might be," "seemed to be"—such language can commit literary murder, as we'll see later on.

Meanwhile, another question popped up: If the story *did* advocate meat-eating, "might it be viewed" (using the Board's language) the opposite way, as an "anti-animal rights" story that could offend 10th graders from vegetarian families? If so, would it be banned with equal rigor? Perhaps not, since in our culture many stories depict people eating meat, or "appearing to" enjoy the act and idea of meat-eating, but are not given the kind of harsh scrutiny that was applied to "Am I Blue?" on tests like this one.

Thus an important lesson about censorship: You can't ban something just because it may or might or could or can offend somebody. One of the strengths of a democracy lies in bringing together many different points of view, any of which will certainly offend one or more persons at some time or another, to get to the truth of a matter. It would be awful, and illegal, thank heaven, if we all had to conform to one way of thinking—that would not be the truth; it would be state-originated propaganda.

Certainly getting at the truth about Alice Walker's stories was the aim of citizens, officials, politicians and Board of Education members alike at a three-hour hearing that grew so emotional an NAACP spokesperson accused the Board of being "lower than Nazis" for withdrawing Walker's work from the tests. English teachers supporting Walker, given a chance to state their views, explained that each story could be interpreted on several levels. For example, "Am I Blue?" they said, could be seen as an allegory in which the abuse of a horse named Blue represents the way people treat the less fortunate among them.

That turned out to be one of many notions. Another was that "Am I Blue?" is the story of slavery replayed in modern times, through an animal's experience, with an African-American woman as witness. When the narrator looks into the eyes of the horse named Blue, who has been bought, penned up, used for stud, betrayed and essentially abandoned, she better understands why Blue and centuries of others who have been enslaved could shut down their feelings and be seen by some as passive and dependent on the status quo of white ownership.

Walker herself "blamed the religious right for objecting to 'Roselily' because its primary character is a black, unwed mother," the *San Francisco Chronicle* wrote. "Calling all unwed mothers 'the most scared and the most sacred' in our society, Walker rose to their defense and asked the privileged Californians . . . to treat them as treasures too."

Others discussed another interpretation: "Roselily" could be viewed as that pivotal moment in everyone's life in which humankind's questioning of God—and of objecting to the injustice in the world that God could so easily resolve but doesn't—is more like the questioning by Job in the Bible than anything simplistically dismissed as "antireligious."

Roselily's doubts about the preacher who stands before her and her future with the authoritarian groom bear the mark of challenged destiny, a phenomenon that "pro-religious" people have wrestled with for millennia. After all, it's the role of religion to help us understand the difference between fate and faith, destiny and free will—differences that "Roselily" beautifully addresses in a few pages.

That Walker could evoke such universal questions in stories about a horse named Blue and an unwed mother named Roselily is testament to her brilliance as a fiction writer, but of course that's exactly what got lost in all the shouting at the Board of Education hearing. Board President McDowell announced, "I do not believe that the actions of the Department of Education's professional staff or of this Board were motivated by racial bias, the intent to exercise censorship, or by pressure from special interest groups of any kind." Now there's an intriguing statement, particularly the part about special interest groups.

It was, in fact, the ultra-conservative Traditional Values Coalition, based in Southern California and led by the Rev. Lou Sheldon, that voiced loud complaints about the Walker stories early on and destroyed the confidentiality of the statewide test after it "leaked the story ["Roselily"] to a southern California newspaper, which published excerpts, prompting letters of protest from Christian conservatives," reported the American Library Association's *Newsletter on Intellectual Freedom.* (That newspaper was the *Riverside Press Enterprise.*)

Groups on the religious right also lobbied the Board of Education about Annie Dillard's "An American Childhood," stating that a snowball fight depicted in that story was too "violent." Here is another case of something that would be hilarious if it weren't so tragic: Pretending that children weren't routinely exposed to the blood-and-guts carnage of war movies, Westerns, cop shows and Saturday morning cartoons, the Board caved in to pressure and withdrew the Dillard story, too.

Thus a second lesson emerges from the fray: Censorship is always arbitrary and always has a secret agenda. Was the religious right really concerned about rural children's sensibilities in the case of "Am I Blue?" or did the Rev. Sheldon's group and others have something else in mind? To answer this question, let's look at the thinking behind statewide tests such as this.

Traditionally, the reason for giving an examination to everyone at once is to allow students to demonstrate—in the form of multiple-choice questions—what they have learned in school about various writers and works by selecting the right fact from a list of possibilities as their answer: Who wrote this, what character said that, and so forth. Tests become standardized and computer-graded; they look and sound very much like the medical questionnaires, job applications or tax returns that students will fill out in later life.

It gradually became apparent, however, that white, middle-class students were doing better at this kind of test than were some minorities, especially African Americans and Latinos. In 1985, for example, the *San Francisco Chronicle* reported that "testing officials say blacks generally score 100 points lower than whites" on Scholastic Aptitude Tests because "the exams require knowledge of such words as 'polo, property taxes and regattas'— words that seem to surface in predominantly white communities more than they do in black or Latino life." At the time, a representative of the SAT's sponsor, the College Board, "agreed that words such as 'oarsmen' and 'pirouette' would be reflective of a certain segment of society," which meant to a director of the NAACP, "for blacks, tests have meant exclusion, rather than inclusion into America's mainstream."

Out of such discussions came the term "culturally biased," meaning that the way knowledge is taught and the way students are tested may be skewed in favor of white experience. "When have you seen a standardized test that said anything about Timbuktu or African authors?" one black pastor asked. "From day one, school is already racist and biased." Thus educators began looking at the way facts are taught and how they are absorbed in different cultures within the United States; they looked at the language, forms and structures of tests to see if the words themselves and the formula of checking off "right" answers appealed to some but flummoxed others.

In California, changes emerged in the approach to both teaching and testing. There was a new commitment to teach children to think. "Literature-based" classes were instituted in which students learned about English by reading actual works of literature rather than duller-than-dull textbooks. Instead of testing what facts students knew, educators geared exams to test what students thought; instead of asking students to check off multiple-choice answers, the tests began asking them to express their thoughts and feelings in essay form. And contrary to what rhetoric against the test would lead us to believe, testers continued to evaluate spelling and punctuation skills with a separate score.

On occasion, instead of asking students to spout back facts they had memorized, the tests presented a piece of literature—a short story or excerpt—to read and respond to right on the page. And if that piece of literature were too difficult (unlike "Am I Blue?" for example, "Roselily" on first reading can be dense and unapproachable for some), students could discuss it in small groups, then return to the test and write their essays, perhaps inspired with new ideas from the group's give-and-take. In this way, the emphasis was removed from learning-by-rote and placed instead on reading, thinking and writing. As the *Los Angeles Times* described it, "Although this new system, called 'performance-based' or 'authentic assessment,' is considerably more expensive to develop and score, educators said it provides a much better method of determining what a student can do and can help shape reforms in teaching and curriculum."

This became, then, the California Learning Assessment System, or CLAS, a test for students in grades 4, 8 and 10. In its attempt to invite students to think and write critically, it is unlike any achievement exam ever conducted in California or most other states. And in its aim to create a level playing field for all students who take it, the test has come under heavy criticism, particularly from conservatives. They denounce CLAS as an invasion of students' privacy and a violation of students' religious beliefs and personal values.

And guess who is out there leading this conservative vanguard: Why it's the Rev. Lou Sheldon—along with his wife Beverly—and their Traditional Values Coalition, which "objected to the new system of testing in general because the group believes it emphasizes 'emotions, not intellect,'" Steve Sheldon, the Sheldons' son, told the *Los Angeles Times*. "It is not the role of the school to test [students] on their feelings," said Beverly Sheldon, who also protested curriculum changes.

For some, what underlies such remarks is the fear that black and Latino kids will have an easier time with CLAS—why, even black unwed mothers might have a chance—because a level playing field has finally and with great effort been achieved for all students in California tests. If Walker's earlier statements are any indication, it's those very students of the "wrong" color and "wrong" background whose eligibility so terrifies the religious right to begin with. This is another lesson the Walker controversy teaches us: Censorship is always motivated by fear.

But didn't we say at the beginning that a funny thing happened to Alice Walker on her way to winning an award? We did, and here's how it turned out: Following the noisy and emotional hearing, the Board of Education reversed its decision. Acting Schools Superintendent Dawson promised to initiate a new method of selecting literary pieces for the CLAS tests and for dealing with complaints so that no one could accuse anybody of censorship from then on. (A hearing was in fact held the following month, at which it seems nothing was accomplished.)

So now let's accompany Alice Walker to the gala Fifth Annual Governor's Arts Awards in Los Angeles at which she, Spielberg, Hockney and Holbrook are all to be feted as the before-mentioned "state treasures." Everyone is in a happy, celebratory mood. Candelabras deck the glittering tables, and for the first time, nobody is symbolically punching out anybody else. Word has it that the actual prize each winner will receive is a foot-high art piece of museum quality. The mood of anticipation and excitement heightens.

And now, the drum roll: Walker's name and award are announced. Amidst great applause and ovation, she glides to the stage to receive the prize, mounts the stairs to the podium—and is handed a gilded statuette of a headless, limbless female body mounted on a bronze base.

By this time, we should note, Walker has moved on to research another area of oppression—that phenomenon in many regions of Africa and the Middle East (and not unknown in the Western Hemisphere) in which young women are subjected to genital mutilation soon after they reach puberty. Walker will go on to both decry this crippling practice and plea for understanding in a film and companion book called *Warrior Marks,* and in a sequel to *The Color Purple* called *Possessing the Secret of Joy.*

This was very much on her mind, then, when she reached the podium to accept her award as a "state treasure" and was stunned to receive the torso statuette. "Imagine my horror when, after four years of thinking about the mutilation of women, I was presented with a decapitated, armless, legless woman, on which my name hung from a chain," she said later. "Though these mutilated figures are prized by museums and considered 'art' by some, the message they deliver is of domination, violence and destruction."

Walker accepted the award with a gracious and eloquent speech—it is not her way to censor other people's idea of art, unlike some we might mention—but in the end, she decided to store the torso in a box. "I would have cherished much more something whole, natural, nonthreatening. A feather found in the forest, a seashell or a stone."

Her mention of "something whole" was not incidental. What makes a person whole in the midst of devastation is a common theme in Alice Walker's work, and indeed it rises up to shock our senses on the first page of her novel, *The Color Purple*. Here is 14-year-old Celie, who's been ordered to "do what your mammy wouldn't," enduring and trying to make sense of repeated rapes and beatings, her first pregnancy and this overwhelming and abiding threat: "You better not never tell nobody but God. It'd kill your mammy." So in a series of letters that weave a brilliantly complicated but simple narrative, Celie pours out her feelings to God. From the moment on the first page when she dares to speak the unspeakable, if "only" to God, Celie's torturous path to freedom begins.

Tellingly, it was the first page that stopped many of the people who wanted to censor *The Color Purple*, thus demonstrating another lesson censorship teaches us—that readers' interpretations are always subjective, and anybody can claim offense at just about anything. Typical of comments was this one by a Tennessee man: "I read just enough of the book to know I don't want to read the book." Others who kept reading believed Walker's novel was filled with "bad language," "profanity," "garbage," "filth," "smut," a "feminist agenda at the expense of black men," "sexual and social explicitness," "troubling ideas about race relations, man's relationship to God, African history and human sexuality" and the "undermining [of] family values."

From the beginning, then, of the novel's publication in 1982, a knee-jerk reaction set in. The book has been pulled from the shelves of schools and libraries all over the country—and that peculiar language of murky meaning, which begins with such words as "might be," "seemed to be" as we noted above, turns even more obscure. "I abhor censorship," a Virginia high school principal said after taking *The Color Purple* out of library circulation. "At the same time, the materials in a public school library are there for a purpose." Really. Well, what other purpose could there be than to support public access to the free and uninterrupted circulation of ideas?

This is why children have become the key to so many censorship fights. People who want to ban books like *The Color Purple* will often say they agree with First Amendment principles, but when it comes to children reading the work in question, they add, all bets are off. "If someone wants to read this book at home on their own, that's up to them," said one North Carolina parent about *The Color Purple*. "But when you take a child who has no choice and tell him he has to read it, that's different."

But why is it different? No student in any school has a choice in what is assigned—that's why books are assigned, not elected, in a place of learning—to help children of one culture learn, through the context of classroom teaching, about people in another culture. Certainly references to God, sex and swear words appear in other assigned works—Shakespeare, the Bible, Chaucer—and books like *The Color Purple* do go through a great deal of screening by educators who weigh the literary quality of each work long before it ends up in the classroom.

This is not, then, a question of looking out for the best interests of children who could easily be exposed to destruction and violence in movies and television, and in some magazines and pornographic books. It's a question, rather, of blaming a book like *The Color Purple*, winner of the Pulitzer Prize and American Book Award, acclaimed internationally as a true masterpiece and one of the most accessible works of fiction ever to be taught in the schools. When a book like this is given credit for literary merit before students ever see it on their list of assigned reading, what, then, is the problem? Why censor it at all?

We don't need to describe the Oregon parents' group that actually cut out all the good parts of Walker's novel (story, characters, theme, subplots, imagery, location) and "condensed" its 295 pages into 1.25 pages of "filth," which showed every instance of the word "fuck" and every description of sex in the novel. It's too silly and again unbelievably tragic since the group then sent the 1.25 pages of seemingly pure profanity to families with an accompanying letter that asked: "Do you think this material lives up to [our city's] standards for academic excellence and moral decency?" Right: A list of swear words and depictions of rape—let's award it the Pulitzer Prize.

But we do need to mention Alice Walker's incredible bravery in the face of enormous and continuing efforts at censorship of her work and criticism of her talent. This is a writer who has almost single-handedly made world audiences aware of issues involving domestic violence, incest and female genital mutilation through an art form we call literature. That we can sample a small but key portion of her work in this book is a worthy education in itself.

Patricia Holt
San Francisco, 1996

17

Roselily

Dearly Beloved,

She dreams; dragging herself across the world. A small girl in her mother's white robe and veil, knee raised waist high through a bowl of quicksand soup. The man who stands beside her is against this standing on the front porch of her house, being married to the sound of cars whizzing by on highway 61.

we are gathered here

Like cotton to be weighed. Her fingers at
the last minute busily removing dry leaves
and twigs. Aware it is a superficial sweep.
She knows he blames Mississippi for the
respectful way the men turn their heads up
in the yard, the women stand waiting and
knowledgeable, their children held from
mischief by teachings from the wrong God.
He glares beyond them to the occupants of
the cars, white faces glued to promises
beyond a country wedding, noses thrust
forward like dogs on a track. For him they
usurp the wedding.

in the sight of God

Yes, open house. That is what country
black folks like. She dreams she does not
already have three children. A squeeze
around the flowers in her hands chokes off
three and four and five years of breath.

Instantly she is ashamed and frightened in her superstition. She looks for the first time at the preacher, forces humility into her eyes, as if she believes he is, in fact, a man of God. She can imagine God, a small black boy, timidly pulling the preacher's coattail.

to join this man and this woman

She thinks of ropes, chains, handcuffs, his religion. His place of worship. Where she will be required to sit apart with covered head. In Chicago, a word she hears when thinking of smoke, from his description of what a cinder was, which they never had in Panther Burn. She sees hovering over the heads of the clean neighbors in her front yard black specks falling, clinging, from the sky. But in Chicago. Respect, a chance to build. Her children at last from underneath the detrimental wheel. A chance to be on top. What a relief, she thinks. What a vision, a view, from up so high.

in holy matrimony.

Her fourth child she gave away to the child's father who had some money. Certainly a good job. Had gone to Harvard. Was a good man but weak because good language meant so much to him he could not live with Roselily. Could not abide TV in the living room, five beds in three rooms, no Bach except from four to six on Sunday afternoons. No chess at all. She does not forget to worry about her son among his father's people. She wonders if the New England climate will agree with him. If he will ever come down to Mississippi, as his father did, to try to right the country's wrongs. She wonders if he will be stronger than his father. His father cried off and on throughout her pregnancy. Went to skin and bones. Suffered nightmares, retching and falling out of bed. Tried to kill himself. Later told his wife he found the right baby through friends. Vouched for, the sterling qualities that would make up his character.

It is not her nature to blame. Still, she is not entirely thankful. She supposes New England, the North, to be quite different from what she knows. It seems right somehow to her that people who move there to live return home completely changed. She thinks of the air, the smoke, the cinders. Imagines cinders big as hailstones; heavy, weighing on the people. Wonders how this pressure finds its way into the veins, roping the springs of laughter.

If there's anybody here that
knows a reason why

But of course they know no reason why
beyond what they daily have come to
know. She thinks of the man who will be
her husband, feels shut away from him
because of the stiff severity of his plain
black suit. His religion. A lifetime of black
and white. Of veils. Covered head. It is as
if her children are already gone from her.
Not dead, but exalted on a pedestal, a stalk
that has no roots. She wonders how to
make new roots. It is beyond her. She wonders what one does with memories in a
brand-new life. This had seemed easy, until
she thought of it. "The reasons why . . . the
people who" . . . she thinks, and does not
wonder where the thought is from.

these two should not be joined

She thinks of her mother, who is dead.
Dead, but still her mother. Joined. This is
confusing. Of her father. A gray old man
who sold wild mink, rabbit, fox skins to
Sears, Roebuck. He stands in the yard, like
a man waiting for a train. Her young sis-
ters stand behind her in smooth green
dresses, with flowers in their hands and
hair. They giggle, she feels, at the absurdity
of the wedding. They are ready for something new. She thinks the man beside her
should marry one of them. She feels old.
Yoked. An arm seems to reach out from
behind her and snatch her backward. She
thinks of cemeteries and the long sleep of
grandparents mingling in the dirt. She
believes that she believes in ghosts. In the
soil giving back what it takes.

together,

In the city. He sees her in a new way. This she knows, and is grateful. But is it new enough? She cannot always be a bride and virgin, wearing robes and veil. Even now her body itches to be free of satin and voile, organdy and lily of the valley. Memories crash against her. Memories of being bare to the sun. She wonders what it will be like. Not to have to go to a job. Not to work in a sewing plant. Not to worry about learning to sew straight seams in workingmen's overalls, jeans, and dress pants. Her place will be in the home, he has said, repeatedly, promising her rest she had prayed for. But now she wonders. When she is rested, what will she do? They will make babies—she thinks practically about her fine brown body, his strong black one. They will be inevitable. Her hands will be full. Full of what? Babies.

She is not comforted.

let him speak

She wishes she had asked him to explain
more of what he meant. But she was impatient. Impatient to be done with sewing.
With doing everything for three children,
alone. Impatient to leave the girls she had
known since childhood, their children
growing up, their husbands hanging
around her, already old, seedy. Nothing
about them that she wanted, or needed.
The fathers of her children driving by,
waving, not waving; reminders of times
she would just as soon forget. Impatient to
see the South Side, where they would live
and build and be respectable and respected
and free. Her husband would free her. A
romantic hush. Proposal. Promises. A new
life! Respectable, reclaimed, renewed. Free!
In robe and veil.

or forever hold

She does not even know if she loves him.
She loves his sobriety. His refusal to sing
just because he knows the tune. She loves
his pride. His blackness and his gray car.
She loves his understanding of her *condition.* She thinks she loves the effort he will
make to redo her into what he truly wants.
His love of her makes her completely con-
scious of how unloved she was before.
This is something; though it makes her
unbearably sad. Melancholy. She blinks her
eyes. Remembers she is finally being married, like other girls. Like other girls,
women? Something strains upward behind
her eyes. She thinks of the something as a
rat trapped, cornered, scurrying to and fro
in her head, peering through the windows
of her eyes. She wants to live for once. But
doesn't know quite what that means.
Wonders if she has ever done it. If she ever

will. The preacher is odious to her. She
wants to strike him out of the way, out of
her light, with the back of her hand. It
seems to her he has always been standing
in front of her, barring her way.

his peace.

The rest she does not hear. She feels a kiss,
passionate, rousing, within the general
pandemonium. Cars drive up blowing
their horns. Firecrackers go off. Dogs come
from under the house and begin to yelp
and bark. Her husband's hand is like the
clasp of an iron gate. People congratulate.
Her children press against her. They look
with awe and distaste mixed with hope at
their new father. He stands curiously apart,
in spite of the people crowding about to
grasp his free hand. He smiles at them all
but his eyes are as if turned inward. He
knows they cannot understand that he is

not a Christian. He will not explain himself. He feels different, he looks it. The old women thought he was like one of their sons except that he had somehow got away from them. Still a son, not a son. Changed.

She thinks how it will be later in the night in the silvery gray car. How they will spin through the darkness of Mississippi and in the morning be in Chicago, Illinois. She thinks of Lincoln, the president. That is all she knows about the place. She feels ignorant, *wrong,* backward. She presses her worried fingers into his palm. He is standing in front of her. In the crush of wellwishing people, he does not look back.

Am I Blue?

"Ain't these tears in these eyes

*tellin' you?"**

For about three years my companion and I rented a small house in the country that stood on the edge of a large meadow that appeared to run from the end of our deck straight into the mountains. The mountains, however, were quite far away, and between us and them there was, in fact, a

*©1929 Warner Bros., Inc. (renewed). By Grant Clarke and Harry Akst. All rights reserved. Used by permission.

town. It was one of the many pleasant aspects of the house that you never really were aware of this.

It was a house of many windows, low, wide, nearly floor to ceiling in the living room, which faced the meadow, and it was from one of these that I first saw our clos- est neighbor, a large white horse, cropping grass, flipping its mane, and ambling about—not over the entire meadow, which stretched well out of sight of the house, but over the five or so fenced-in acres that were next to the twenty-odd that we had rented. I soon learned that the horse, whose name was Blue, belonged to a man who lived in another town, but was boarded by our neighbor next door. Occasionally, one of the children, usually a stocky teen-ager, but sometimes a much younger girl or boy, could be seen riding Blue. They would appear in the meadow, climb up on his back, ride furiously for ten or fifteen minutes, then get off, slap Blue on the flanks, and not be seen again for a month or more.

There were many apple trees in our yard, and one by the fence that Blue could almost reach. We were soon in the habit of feeding him apples, which he relished, especially because by the middle of summer the meadow grasses—so green and succulent since January—had dried out from lack of rain, and Blue stumbled about munching the dried stalks half-heartedly. Sometimes he would stand very still just by the apple tree, and when one of us came out he would whinny, snort loudly, or stamp the ground. This meant, of course: I want an apple.

It was quite wonderful to pick a few apples, or collect those that had fallen to the ground overnight, and patiently hold them, one by one, up to his large, toothy mouth. I remained as thrilled as a child by his flexible dark lips, huge, cubelike teeth that crunched the apples, core and all, with such finality, and his high, broad-breasted *enormity*; beside which, I felt small indeed. When I was a child, I used to ride horses, and was especially friendly with one named Nan until the day I was riding and my brother deliberately spooked her and I was thrown, head first, against the trunk of a tree. When I came to, I was in bed and my mother was bending worriedly over me; we silently agreed that perhaps horse-back riding was not the safest sport for me. Since then I have walked, and prefer walking to horseback riding—but I had forgotten the depth of feeling one could see in horses' eyes.

I was therefore unprepared for the expression in Blue's. Blue was lonely. Blue was horribly lonely and bored. I was not shocked that this should be the case; five acres to tramp by yourself, endlessly, even in the most beautiful of meadows—and his was—cannot provide many interesting events, and once rainy season turned to dry that was about it. No, I was shocked that I had forgotten that human animals and nonhuman animals can communicate quite well; if we are brought up around animals as children we take this for granted. By the time we are adults we no longer remember. However, the animals have not changed. They are in fact *completed* creations (at least they seem to be, so much more than we) who are not likely *to* change; it is their nature to express themselves. What else are they going to express? And they do. And, generally speaking, they are ignored.

After giving Blue the apples, I would wander back to the house, aware that he was observing me. Were more apples not forthcoming then? Was that to be his sole entertainment for the day? My partner's small son had decided he wanted to learn how to piece a quilt; we worked in silence on our respective squares as I thought . . .

Well, about slavery: about white children, who were raised by black people, who knew their first all-accepting love from black women, and then, when they were twelve or so, were told they must "forget" the deep levels of communication between themselves and "mammy" that they knew. Later they would be able to relate quite calmly, "My old mammy was sold to another good family." "My old mammy was --- ---." Fill in the blank. Many more years later a white woman would say: "I can't understand these Negroes, these blacks. What do they want? They're so different from us."

And about the Indians, considered to be "like animals" by the "settlers" (a very benign euphemism for what they actually were), who did not understand their description as a compliment.

And about the thousands of American men who marry Japanese, Korean, Filipina, and other non-English-speaking women and of how happy they report they are, *"blissfully,"* until their brides learn to speak English, at which point the marriages tend to fall apart. What then did the men see, when they looked into the eyes of the women they married, before they could speak English? Apparently only their own reflections.

I thought of society's impatience with the young. "Why are they playing the music so loud?" Perhaps the children have listened to much of the music of oppressed people their parents danced to before they were born, with its passionate but soft cries for acceptance and love, and they have wondered why their parents failed to hear.

I do not know how long Blue had inhabited his five beautiful, boring acres before we moved into our house; a year after we had arrived—and had also traveled to other valleys, other cities, other worlds— he was still there.

But then, in our second year at the house, something happened in Blue's life. One morning, looking out the window at the fog that lay like a ribbon over the meadow, I saw another horse, a brown one, at the other end of Blue's field. Blue appeared to be afraid of it, and for several days made no attempt to go near. We went away for a week. When we returned, Blue had decided to make friends and the two horses ambled or galloped along together, and Blue did not come nearly as often to the fence underneath the apple tree.

When he did, bringing his new friend with him, there was a different look in his eyes. A look of independence, of self-possession, of inalienable *horse*ness. His friend eventually became pregnant. For months and months there was, it seemed to me, a mutual feeling between me and the horses of justice, of peace. I fed apples to them both. The look in Blue's eyes was one of unabashed "this is *it*ness."

It did not, however, last forever. One day, after a visit to the city, I went out to give Blue some apples. He stood waiting, or so I thought, though not beneath the tree. When I shook the tree and jumped back from the shower of apples, he made no move. I carried some over to him. He managed to half-crunch one. The rest he let fall to the ground. I dreaded looking into his eyes—because I had of course noticed that Brown, his partner, had gone—but I did look. If I had been born into slavery, and my partner had been sold or killed, my eyes would have looked like that. The children next door explained that Blue's partner had been "put with him" (the same expression that old people used, I had noticed, when speaking of an ancestor during slavery who had been impregnated by her owner) so that they could mate and she conceive. Since that was accomplished, she had been taken back by her owner, who lived somewhere else.

Will she be back? I asked.

They didn't know.

Blue was like a crazed person. Blue *was*, to me, a crazed person. He galloped furiously, as if he were being ridden, around and around his beautiful five acres. He whinnied until he couldn't. He tore at the ground with his hooves. He butted himself against his single shade tree. He looked always and always toward the road down which his partner had gone. And then, occasionally, when he came up for apples, or I took apples to him, he looked at me. It was a look so piercing, so full of grief, a look so *human*, I almost laughed (I felt too sad to cry) to think there are people who do not know that animals suffer. People like me who have forgotten, and daily forget, all that animals try to tell us. "Everything you do to us will happen to you; we are your teachers, as you are ours. We are one lesson" is essentially it, I think. There are those who never once have even considered animals' rights: those who have been taught that animals actually want to be used and abused by us, as small children "love" to be frightened, or women "love" to be mutilated and raped . . . . They are the great-grandchildren of those who honestly thought, because someone taught them this: "Women can't think," and "niggers can't faint." But most disturbing of all, in Blue's large brown eyes was a new look, more painful than the look of despair: the look of disgust with human beings, with life; the look of hatred. And it was odd what the look of hatred did. It gave him, for the first time, the look of a beast. And what that meant was that he had put up a barrier within to protect himself from further violence; all the apples in the world wouldn't change that fact.

And so Blue remained, a beautiful part of our landscape, very peaceful to look at from the window, white against the grass. Once a friend came to visit and said, looking out on the soothing view: "And it *would* have to be a *white* horse; the very image of freedom." And I thought, yes, the animals are forced to become for us merely "images" of what they once so beautifully expressed. And we are used to drinking milk from containers showing "contented" cows, whose real lives we want to hear nothing about, eating eggs and drumsticks from "happy" hens, and munching hamburgers advertised by bulls of integrity who seem to command their fate.

As we talked of freedom and justice one day for all, we sat down to steaks. I am eating misery, I thought, as I took the first bite. And spit it out.

The Color Purple

AN EXCERPT

*You better not never tell nobody but God. It'd
kill your mammy.*

Dear God,

I am fourteen years old. ~~I am~~ I have
always been a good girl. Maybe you can
give me a sign letting me know what is
happening to me.

Last spring after little Lucious come I
heard them fussing. He was pulling on her
arm. She say It too soon, Fonso, I ain't
well. Finally he leave her alone. A week go
by, he pulling on her arm again. She say
Naw, I ain't gonna. Can't you see I'm
already half dead, an all of these chilren.

She went to visit her sister doctor over
Macon. Left me to see after the others. He

46

never had a kine word to say to me. Just say You gonna do what your mammy wouldn't. First he put his thing up gainst my hip and sort of wiggle it around. Then he grab hold my titties. Then he push his thing inside my pussy. When that hurt, I cry. He start to choke me, saying You better shut up and git used to it.

But I don't never git used to it. And now I feels sick every time I be the one to cook. My mama she fuss at me an look at me. She happy, cause he good to her now. But too sick to last long.

Dear God,

My mama dead. She die screaming and cussing. She scream at me. She cuss at me. I'm big. I can't move fast enough. By time I git back from the well, the water be warm. By time I git the tray ready the food be cold. By time I git all the children ready for school it be dinner time. He don't say nothing. He set there by the bed holding her hand an cryin, talking bout don't leave me, don't go.

She ast me bout the first one Whose it is? I say God's. I don't know no other man or what else to say. When I start to hurt and then my stomach start moving and then that little baby come out my pussy chewing on it fist you could have knock me over with a feather.

Don't nobody come see us.

She got sicker an sicker.

Finally she ast Where it is?

I say God took it.

He took it. He took it while I was sleeping.
Kilt it out there in the woods. Kill this one
too, if he can.

Dear God,

He act like he can't stand me no more. Say I'm evil an always up to no good. He took my other little baby, a boy this time. But I don't think he kilt it. I think he sold it to a man an his wife over Monticello. I got breasts full of milk running down myself. He say Why don't you look decent? Put on something. But what I'm sposed to put on? I don't have nothing.

I keep hoping he fine somebody to marry. I see him looking at my little sister. She scared. But I say I'll take care of you. With God help.

Dear God,

He come home with a girl from round Gray. She be my age but they married. He be on her all the time. She walk round like she don't know what hit her. I think she thought she love him. But he got so many of us. All needing somethin.

My little sister Nettie is got a boyfriend in the same shape almost as Pa. His wife died. She was kilt by her boyfriend coming home from church. He got only three children though. He seen Nettie in church and now every Sunday evening here come Mr. _____. I tell Nettie to keep at her books. It be more then a notion taking care of children ain't even yourn. And look what happen to Ma.

Dear God,

He beat me today cause he say I winked at a boy in church. I may have got somethin in my eye but I didn't wink. I don't even look at mens. That's the truth. I look at women, tho, cause I'm not scared of them. Maybe cause my mama cuss me you think I kept mad at her. But I ain't. I felt sorry for mama. Trying to believe his story kilt her.

Sometime he still be looking at Nettie, but I always git in his light. Now I tell her to marry Mr. _____. I don't tell her why.

I say Marry him, Nettie, an try to have one good year out your life. After that, I know she be big.

But me, never again. A girl at church say you git big if you bleed every month. I don't bleed no more.

Dear God,

Mr. _____ finally come right out an ast for Nettie hand in marriage. But He won't let her go. He say she too young, no experience. Say Mr. _____ got too many children already. Plus What about the scandal his wife cause when somebody kill her? And what about all this stuff he hear bout Shug Avery? What bout that?

I ast our new mammy bout Shug Avery. What it is? I ast. She don't know but she say she gon fine out.

She do more then that. She git a picture. The first one of a real person I ever seen. She say Mr. _____ was taking somethin out his billfold to show Pa an it fell out an slid under the table. Shug Avery was a woman. The most beautiful woman I ever saw. She more pretty then my mama. She bout ten thousand times more prettier then me. I see her there in furs. Her face rouge. Her hair like somethin tail. She grinning with her foot up on somebody motocar. Her eyes serious tho. Sad some.

I ast her to give me the picture. An all night long I stare at it. An now when I dream, I dream of Shug Avery. She be dress to kill, whirling and laughing.

Dear God,

I ast him to take me instead of Nettie while our new mammy sick. But he just ast me what I'm talking bout. I tell him I can fix myself up for him. I duck into my room and come out wearing horsehair, feathers, and a pair of our new mammy high heel shoes. He beat me for dressing trampy but he do it to me anyway.

Mr. _____ come that evening. I'm in the bed crying. Nettie she finally see the light of day, clear. Our new mammy she see it too. She in her room crying. Nettie tend to first one, then the other. She so scared she go out doors and vomit. But not out front where the two mens is.

Mr. _____ say, Well Sir, I sure hope you done change your mind.

He say, Naw, Can't say I is.

Mr. _____ say, Well, you know, my poor little ones sure could use a mother.

Well, He say, real slow, I can't let you have Nettie. She too young. Don't know nothing but what you tell her. Sides, I want her to git some more schooling. Make a school-teacher out of her. But I can let you have Celie. She the oldest anyway. She ought to marry first. She ain't fresh tho, but I spect you know that. She spoiled. Twice. But you don't need a fresh woman no how. I got a fresh one in there myself and she sick all the time. He spit, over the railing. The children git on her nerve, she not much of a cook. And she big already.

Mr. _____ he don't say nothing. I stop crying I'm so surprise.

She ugly. He say. But she ain't no stranger to hard work. And she clean. And God done fixed her. You can do everything just like you want to and she ain't gonna make you feed it or clothe it.

Mr. _____ still don't say nothing. I take out the picture of Shug Avery. I look into her eyes. Her eyes say Yeah, it *bees* that way sometime.

Fact is, he say, I got to git rid of her. She too old to be living here at home. And she a bad influence on my other girls. She'd come with her own linen. She can take that cow she raise down there back of the crib. But Nettie you flat out can't have. Not now. Not never.

Mr. _____ finally speak. Clearing his throat. I ain't never really look at that one, he say.

Well, next time you come you can look at her. She ugly. Don't even look like she kin to Nettie. But she'll make the better wife.

She ain't smart either, and I'll just be fair, you have to watch her or she'll give away everything you own. But she can work like a man.

Mr. _____ say How old she is?

He say, She near twenty. And another thing—She tell lies.

Dear God,

It took him the whole spring, from March
to June, to make up his mind to take me.
All I thought about was Nettie. How she
could come to me if I marry him and he be
so love struck with her I could figure out a
way for us to run away. Us both be hitting
Nettie's schoolbooks pretty hard, cause us
know we got to be smart to git away. I
know I'm not as pretty or as smart as
Nettie, but *she* say I ain't dumb.

The way you know who discover America,
Nettie say, is think bout cucumbers. That
what Columbus sound like. I learned all
about Columbus in first grade, but look
like he the first thing I forgot. She say
Columbus come here in boats call the
Neater, the Peter, and the Santomareater.
Indians so nice to him he force a bunch of

'em back home with him to wait on the queen.

But it hard to think with gitting married to Mr. _____ hanging over my head.

The first time I got big Pa took me out of school. He never care that I love it. Nettie stood there at the gate holding tight to my hand. I was all dress for first day. You too dumb to keep going to school, Pa say. Nettie the clever one in this bunch.

But Pa, Nettie say, crying, Celie smart too. Even Miss Beasley say so. Nettie dote on Miss Beasley. Think nobody like her in the world.

Pa say, Whoever listen to anything Addie Beasley have to say. She run off at the mouth so much no man would have her. That how come she have to teach school. He never look up from cleaning his gun. Pretty soon a bunch of white mens come walking cross the yard. They have guns too.

Pa git up and follow 'em. The rest of the week I vomit and dress wild game.

But Nettie never give up. Next thing I know Miss Beasley at our house trying to talk to Pa. She say long as she been a teacher she never know nobody want to learn bad as Nettie and me. But when Pa call me out and she see how tight my dress is, she stop talking and go.

Nettie still don't understand. I don't neither. All us notice is I'm all the time sick and fat.

I feel bad sometime Nettie done pass me in learnin. But look like nothing she say can git in my brain and stay. She try to tell me something bout the ground not being flat. I just say, Yeah, like I know it. I never tell her how flat it look to me.

Mr. _____ come finally one day looking all drug out. The woman he had helping him done quit. His mammy done said No More.

He say, Let me see her again.

Pa call me. *Celie,* he say. Like it wasn't nothing. Mr. _____ want another look at you.

I go stand in the door. The sun shine in my eyes. He's still up on his horse. He look me up and down.

Pa rattle his newspaper. Move up, he won't bite, he say.

I go closer to the steps, but not too close cause I'm a little scared of his horse.

Turn round, Pa say.

I turn round. One of my little brothers come up. I think it was Lucious. He fat and playful, all the time munching on something.

He say, What you doing that for?

Pa say, Your sister thinking bout marriage.

Didn't mean nothing to him. He pull my dresstail and ast can he have some blackberry jam out the safe.

I say, Yeah.

She good with children, Pa say, rattling his paper open more. Never heard her say a hard word to nary one of them. Just give 'em everything they ast for, is the only problem.

Mr. _____ say, That cow still coming?

He say, Her cow.

APPENDICES

NOTE: *The following appendices are comprised of representative selections of the debates surrounding Alice Walker's work. Appendix A presents both selections from the print media's contributions to the debate over the CLAS test and a significant portion of the statements made at the California State Board of Education's public hearing about the removal of the stories. Appendix B presents a brief overview of various (and ongoing) attempts to ban or suppress* The Color Purple *and arguments about that novel's treatment of African-American men and human sexuality.* **Readers interested in obtaining a pamphlet containing full transcripts of both the State Board of Education Meeting and the California State Assembly Education Committee hearing, as well as a more extensive range of materials on attempts to ban** The Color Purple, *should write or call Aunt Lute Books (see final page).*

APPENDIX A:
The CLAS Exam Controversy

In the Newspapers

On March 10, 1994, the day before the State Board of Education met to discuss the removal of the stories from the CLAS exam, the San Francisco Chronicle *reprinted "Am I Blue?" and expressed an interest in hearing readers' reactions to the story. The response was enormous; the* Chronicle *received over six hundred letters, running approximately nine to one "in support of the story, and against the Board of Education's removal of it." Of these, the* Chronicle *printed sixteen, running approximately nine to seven in favor of "Am I Blue?" and eleven to five opposed to the Board's actions (that is, not everyone who opposed the Board's actions did so on the grounds of liking the story). The following letters are representative of the range of opinions expressed, if not the ratio.*

Editor—Regarding Alice Walker's "Blue," right in the center, the very navel of this pedestrian, uncreative remembrance dressed up as a story, the one italicized word in the story, "enormity," is used wrong—the kind of blooper a pretentious pseudo-literary high schooler would make. Could it be the PC empress has no clothes? Is this affirmative action as applied to literature?

As for the cries of censorship by the litleft, imagine the outcry for proscription if a test story were deemed slighting of minorities.
MICHAEL SHERRELL
Sebastopol

Editor—Thank you for the opportunity to read Alice Walker's short story "Am I Blue?" After reading it I feel a bit clearer about the tremendous amount of controversy surrounding this very short story. "Am I Blue?" is a very skillfully drawn emotional poke at many subjects that range from slavery, racism, women's rights, general insensitivity, and of course, meat eating. The emotion-based view so eloquently expressed in this writing has, not surprisingly, elicited an emotional response from those that disagree with her, particularly the religious right. It is said that they object to the portrayal of meat eating, although I suspect that the real "meat" they are complaining about lies in the body of the essay and not in the final sentence as they claim. Conservative religion would find many prickly issues addressed by Ms. Walker's writing and meat eating is the least thorny of them all.
BRUCE GROSJEAN
San Francisco

Editor—If an excerpt from "Little Black Sambo" was on school tests, and the NAACP petitioned to have it removed (which they would certainly have a right to do), I get the feeling that Alice Walker would not accuse them of censorship and that she would not oppose their

actions. Let's face it. The issue here is not censorship but judgment. I think that board members erred in removing the stories. But I also think it's both dishonest and dangerous to cry censorship whenever someone exercises judgment. After all, The Chronicle doesn't print all my letters. Does that entitle me to accuse them of censorship? I don't think so.
BILL McGREGOR
Berkeley

Editor—The world is full of hate and cruelty and suffering. Alice Walker's "Am I Blue?" represents a look into the eyes of the innocent creatures, the innocent victims, of man's indifference, not only toward animals but toward other humans. Is it uncomfortable to look into the eyes of those who are suffering? Yes. And maybe it's easier to eat animals if you don't think of them as having feelings, families and the ability to experience pain. If this story makes people feel uncomfortable, it's only because it provokes one to think about issues that we may have become desensitized to.

"Am I Blue?" is a brilliant piece of work by one of the most important writers of our time. To withhold this masterpiece from our children for the reason that it is "anti-meat eating," is an embarrassment to all involved. But not as embarrassing as our governor, now denying involvement in the decision to censor.

By the way, I gave up eating meat in 1987. It had nothing to do with reading "Am I Blue?" but it had everything to do with the fact that I no longer felt comfortable eating my friends. I am healthier and happier now and envy people who make the decision earlier in their lives.

Thank you for printing "Am I Blue?" so everyone can decide for themselves if this is a work that should be censored or not.
KAREN BENZEL
Alameda

69

Editor—Why on earth was this story included in the test in the first place? "Am I Blue?" is a wooden, clumsy piece of writing, with a thin and rather sentimental story that staggers and finally disappears under a load of rhetoric. Walker has done much beautiful work, but this story isn't part of it. My guess is that the test-makers chose "Am I Blue?" not because it is the best, most thought-provoking story they could find, but because they wanted to be politically correct in including work by a black female writer. That doesn't excuse the school board's censorship, but it may help explain it.

It's hard to know what to think of their "anti-meat eating" complaint. Can they possibly believe that children are so hypersensitive they'd be rendered incompetent by guilt when they read the last couple of lines in "Am I Blue?" Or are they reacting to the not-so-hidden political reasons for choosing the story in the first place, and just afraid of the flack they'd get if they rejected it because they don't like its other, more controversial messages?

I don't know which is worse, the board's misuse of their power in censoring "Am I Blue?," their indifference to (or ignorance of) literary quality, or their truly bizarre notions about children's sensibilities.

As for Pete Wilson, no new piece of smarmy cynicism from him should surprise us. Shame, shame on the lot of them.
NEVA BEACH
San Francisco

Editor—Thanks for publishing Alice Walker's story—undeniably the best possible information the public could have with which to judge the state's action. I think it's a lovely story, rich with the kind of imaginings and acting-outs that young people do in the process of growing up and learning to make sense of the world. It's certainly not anything I would want to "protect" my own 10th-grader

from; in fact, I'd much rather see him read stories like
that than some of what he does read.

By the way, I hate to get technical, but the ham-
burger is a metaphor, as is the horse. The child in the
story understands this; too bad the Board of Education
missed it.
PETER MAGNANI
San Francisco

On March 20, 1994, the San Jose Mercury News *reprinted
"Roselily" in its "Perspectives" section and invited Beverly
Sheldon of the Traditional Values Coalition and Edward
Kleinschmidt, a poet who teaches creative writing at Santa
Clara University, to respond to the use of the story on the
CLAS test. Sheldon's article, taking up what the* Mercury
*dubbed the "Con" position, repeated more or less what she said
at the State Board of Education meeting. Kleinschmidt's essay,
which occupied the "Pro" position, is reprinted here.*

We all want to have our beliefs challenged

by Edward Kleinschmidt

Congress shall make

I think we can all dream with Roselily, we who are
human, that is, we humans who have, at times, about as
much of the divine in us as a pound of divinity does.
There is no law that I know of, no law on any of the
books, even ones that have been burned through and
through, over and over, until all we have left to read is
the ash, even books in bonfire that warms the hands and
feet of book burners—there is no law that bans dreams.
We can dream on the park bench and not get arrested. We
can dream in the privacy of our cars and not get pulled
over. What would the cop say on the ticket: excessive

dreaming? And we continue to dream, even now holding newsprint in our hands, our fingers a bit darker where truths have rubbed.

no law

This is a test. This is only a test. The real thing will happen later. The real thing is called life. And then there's death, and then there's after life, and then there's after death, and then there's . . . But this, this is only a test. And who flunked the test?

   I've taught 10th graders, and one thing I know about them is that while incredible changes are going on in their bodies and minds, they are confused about those changes. Roselily expresses her own heartfelt quandaries, uncertainties, doubts, dilemmas, and deals with them fearlessly and forthrightly. She doesn't pull a pistol from her pocketbook to solve any differences, as happens between Croat and Serb, Celt and Brit, Sunni and Shiite, Jew and Arab. Has the Traditional Values Coalition branded these actions as "anti-religious"?

respecting

Q. What year was "The Pledge of Allegiance" written?
A. "The Pledge of Allegiance" was written in 1892.
Q. What year was "under God" added to the "Pledge of Allegiance" by an Act of Congress?
A. "Under God" was added by an Act of Congress in 1954.
Respond in 100 words:
Were we, as a nation, without Him/Her for the 178 years prior?

an establishment of religion,

Is there anybody here? *If there's anybody here that knows a reason why* "Roselily" *should* not *be part of a test, raise your hand, then take that hand and cover your face in shame.*

"The serious novelist will write," Alice Walker notes in her book, "In Search of Our Mothers' Gardens," about Flannery O'Connor's stance toward writing, "not what other people want, and certainly not what other people expect, but whatever interests her or him. And that the direction taken, therefore, will be away from sociology, away from the 'writing of explanation,' of 'statistics,' and further into mystery, poetry, and into prophecy.

"What is always needed in the appreciation of art, or life, is the larger perspective. Connections made, or at least attempted, where none existed before, the straining to encompass in one's glance at the varied world the common thread, the unifying theme through immense diversity, a fearlessness of growth, of search, of looking, that enlarges the private and public world. And yet, in our particular society, it is the narrowed and narrowing view of life that often wins.

"If there is one thing African-Americans and Native Americans have retained of their African and ancient American heritage, it is probably the belief that everything is inhabited by spirit."

or

Or is it art? Does it educate? If you give them prayer in the school, the next thing you know we'll be getting algebra shoved down our throats in the churches, multiplication tables set up at the church bazaar.

It was long ago time to sink that unseaworthy vessel, censorship. Yes, we would rescue the censors crowding into the lifeboats. Retrain them. Give tests!

prohibiting the free

Will Roselily be aghast at a Koran on the coffee table when she moves to Chicago? Who of us is annoyed at the Bible in the bedside drawer, the Talmud on the TV stand? Alice Walker's story, her critics say, questions marriage and religion. Don't we also need to question divorce and despair?

73

exercise

Do you think this is a story about religion or a story about the South?

Do you think the preacher represents religion or the patriarchal South?

Comment on the image of God as a small black boy tugging the sleeve of the preacher.

Do you prefer the old 10th grade standby "Silas Marner"?

What we need is for *all* of us to take this test. Gov. Pete Wilson could administer it to us right now, or perhaps wait until the November election, after which he may be applying for the state School Superintendent job. We all want—we demand—to have our beliefs and ideas challenged.

Can we test the supporters of the Traditional Values Coalition for mental incompetence?

thereof, or abridging the

Perhaps the Traditional Values Coalition's fiction masks their real intention: to bring back the multiple choice test the present test replaced, even though studies have shown that these tests lead to multiple personality disorders. Having one and a half million California students write real essays in response to something they read might encourage them to think; reading literature, most experts agree, is a dangerous thing to do; discussing it is more so; writing it can be one step away from condemnation, or from the Pulitzer Prize, as in the case of Alice Walker and Annie Dillard case (also banned from the California test).

freedom of **speech**

Amen!

State Board of Education Meeting

*At its March 11th meeting, the California State Board of
Education conducted a public hearing about its decision to
remove Walker's and Dillard's stories from the 1994 CLAS
exam, listening to arguments from approximately forty speakers representing a wide range of views. Marion McDowell,
President of the State Board of Education, opened the meeting
with a prepared statement, defending the Board's actions
against charges of censorship and racism with a flat-out denial:
"I do not believe that the actions of the Department of
Education's professional staff or of this Board were motivated
by racial bias, the intent to exercise censorship, or by pressure
from special interest groups of any kind . . . . It is truly unfor-
tunate that some have chosen to characterize our actions as
reflecting bias, racism, censorship, or yielding to pressure. The
characterization is simply not true, and is not supported by any
facts of which I am aware . . . . We oppose censorship and racial
bias of any kind, and we strongly encourage all teachers—
particularly teachers of English-language arts—to present
California's public school students with writings, thinking, and
ideas that truly reflect the diversity of our state and society."
After McDowell's opening remarks, the Department of
Education was given thirty minutes to explain the process by
which the CLAS test was developed and specific items for the
test were chosen. Before anyone spoke, Joseph R. Symkowick,
General Counsel for the Board, reminded all speakers that the
test was copyrighted and confidential, and that only general
references should be made to the content of the test. After intro-
ductory remarks by William Dawson (Acting School
Superintendent), Department of Education staff member Dale
Carlson outlined the process of test development. That process,
to which many of the speakers at the public hearing later
referred, included the subjection of both literary selections and
test prompts to a "Balanced Treatment Review" by a committee
composed of individuals reflecting the state's diversity, not educational specialists. It also included extensive field-testing of*

both selections and prompts, so that the bias review committee had at its disposal information about how real students responded to the material. Immediately after the public hearing, and with no discernible discussion, the Board unanimously requested that the Department of Education restore the works in question to the pool of literature selections for future CLAS tests. The California State Assembly Education Committee met the following week to conduct a hearing both to investigate the removal of the stories and to hear testimony about the exam itself. Many of the same speakers appeared, but because Members of the Assembly were able to ask questions, that meeting had a more dialogic, and at times more heated, character than the Board of Education's public hearing. (A transcript of the Assembly hearing is available through Aunt Lute Books).

The following are the statements of approximately half of the speakers who appeared before the State Board of Education during its public hearing. Speakers were allowed two minutes to speak, with a one-minute grace period. Anyone who wished to yield his or her time to another speaker was allowed to do so. The selection of speakers that follows approximates both the range of views expressed at the hearing, as well as the ratio of those who approved of the Board's actions to those who did not. Not represented are those who addressed their comments solely to the CLAS test as an assessment device and not to the Board's decision. The statements represented here were transcribed from audio tapes; every effort has been made to represent the speakers' words accurately and to spell proper names correctly.

Dorothy Erlich— Good morning President McDowell, Dr. Dawson, members of the School Board. My name is Dorothy Erlich; I'm the Executive Director of the ACLU of Northern California. Thank you for giving me an opportunity to speak to you this morning. I must say, I expected to learn more this morning. I expected to understand better why it is it's being said that the story "Roselily" was not removed for ideological reasons. I have heard no evidence that it wasn't removed for that reason. The original statements from the Department suggested that it was. We have filed a Public Records Access Request on Monday, asking this Department, the School Board, the Governor's office, and other public officials to turn over documents, which they are required to do under law, so we can find out the real facts. But I can tell you in the meantime that I am not reassured to find that even if you claim after the fact that it wasn't done, that at least "Roselily" wasn't removed for ideological reasons, it still does seem to be the case that ideas can be held hostage. If a particular group can find someone in the Department who will reveal to them on the telephone what a story is, all they have to do is call a reporter, report what that story is, and we won't have that story in future tests. That's no way to run a school department. I must also say that we came to suggest to you that you develop rules and that you follow those rules and that criteria be established. And we asked, in our Public Records Access Request, to understand better what those rules are. Well I'm happy to see them supplied to us today, and I think, offhand, they're quite impressive. What's most disturbing is that those rules aren't being followed. And that is something that has to be addressed today. I was . . . I found it ironic that we talked today about asking students to think deeply about important matters. And I find that if that is the test, that educators in this state, the School Board, members of this Department, are not thinking deeply about critical matters, and you have failed the test. And the reason that you have failed it, and the reason it's so important, is that you are the guardians, you are the public officials that have the responsibility to secure freedom of expression. You have the responsibility to protect students from censorship, and it feels as though you have failed to do that, and that is a very important task. We must build back the trust in this Department in order to ensure that this can never happen again. And I must say that you have given

us an opportunity to do that. I think that the voices
you're hearing over the last two weeks, the voices that
you will hear today, the voices of organizations who
deeply oppose censorship, the voices of students and parents, educators, artists, writers, who are speaking out on
this issue, gives you some idea of the commitment that
we have to stop censorship in this state, and to send a
warning that it will not be accepted, whether it's inside
the Department or outside the Department. Thank you
very much.

Gloria Mata Tuckman— I'd like to thank the members of
the Board, the State Board of Education, for inviting me
to speak here before you on this controversial matter—an
educationally pivotal issue—this morning. I'm Gloria
Mata Tuckman, president of the Tustin School Board,
founder of the Campaign for California's Kids; presiden-
tial appointee to three national committees; reform
boards; a thirty-year first grade teacher in Santa Ana
Unified, racially diverse schools; a mother of two; a can-
didate for State Superintendent of Public Instruction; and
I'm here also as a citizen of this state of California.

I flew here today from Southern California to
demonstrate my solidarity with the Board's courageous
decision to remove pages of literary excerpts written by
Alice Walker and Annie Dillard from a state assessment
test. While I have nothing but praise and admiration and
respect for the talent and work of these two independent,
strong women, I must take off my hat to you for stepping
up to the plate, and demonstrating your willingness to
take a hit from California's politically correct amen chorus,
all for the sake of the education of California's kids. I suggest the critics of your decision, and most of them are
politicians, spend more time volunteering to teach a child
to read, write, or comprehend a mathematical equation
than playing politics here in Sacramento. I teach for a living; it's my job, five days a week, day in and day out, and
let me tell you, taking the Walker and Dillard excerpts

out of the test isn't what made this controversy political. It was putting the excerpts in that did it. As a teacher in the classroom 180 days a year, I'm here to testify what we need more is more accountability in the classroom, not less. We need more of it from our tests, from our teachers, from our students, and from our California parents.

And I'd like to touch on two points regarding the CLAS test and what's become known as the "Walker controversy." Removing the excerpts from the test was not an act of censorship; it was an act of educational and test-giving responsibility. Students were never prevented from gaining access to either Walker's or Dillard's books, nor were they prevented from checking the Walker or Dillard books out of the library, nor were the books ever removed from the library or classroom shelves. In short, students were never kept from investigating what this flak was all about, because that, my friends, is censorship. The works were removed from the test for what I consider the right reasons. They did not enhance the educational evaluation of California's kids, and that is the sole purpose of the CLAS test. The fact that the questions on the CLAS test that pertained to the Walker and Dillard excerpts ask such nebulous and unspecific questions as "How does this make you feel? Give me your thoughts . . ." Well, let me tell you, I give tests every day, and I give real grades and real evaluations. And let me tell you, it's no way to identify where the student is academically weak or where the student is intellectually strong, which means the test questions are rendered useless, and the students' most fundamental weaknesses are never attended to, and their greatest strengths are never encouraged. Thank you.

Jean Hessburg— Good morning Dr. McDowell and members of the Board of Education. My name is Jean Hessburg. I'm the California Director of People for the American Way, and I'm here today on behalf of the forty thousand California members of our organization to speak in opposition to the removal of "Roselily" and two other stories from the CLAS exam. People for the American Way believes strongly in a public education system in which text books, curricula, and other materials are selected for sound educational and pedagogical reasons, and in which censorship and religious and ideological pressure have no role. We are deeply disturbed by the reported circumstances under which "Roselily" and the other stories were removed from the exam, and by the conflicting reasons that the Department of Education and the Board of Education have since given. Despite the Board's recent news releases asserting that "Roselily" was removed from the exam because the confidentiality of the test had been compromised, the fact remains that in the initial press reports about the incident the Department of Education admitted that it had removed the story based upon objections from the Traditional Values Coalition, an extremist pressure group, over complaints that the story is "anti-religious." Furthermore, sectarian pressure was being exerted even before this press account of the test and apparently led to the *Riverside Press Enterprise* article. The fact also remains that the TVC then publicly expressed its pleasure over the removal of that story and wondered what other stories might be in there.

We're concerned that the reasons for the removal of "Roselily" now being put forth by the Board and the Department may be nothing more than an after-the-fact realization. Although the Board is now claiming the story was removed because of public disclosure, it is our understanding that the committee of experts responsible for developing the test is in fact opposed to deleting material from the exam even though it has been publicly disclosed, so that censors are not given a ready means to sabotage the test. Additional information has recently come to light that further indicates that the Department has not been fully forthcoming about its response to activist pressure. We have learned that the Department has reportedly allowed at least one school board, the

Saddleback School District, to opt out of the exam, and that opt outs are reportedly being sought by other districts under pressure from Phyllis Schlafly's political organization, the Eagle Forum. Given what the press has reported and the Department has admitted, those of us fighting to prevent censorship in our public schools are justifiably concerned about whether the Department and the Board are making decisions based upon ideological rather than pedagogical reasons. Censorship has no place in our public education system. We call upon the Department and the Board to adopt all appropriate procedures to ensure that the content and the conduct of the examination are determined by educational reasons and not by religious and ideological pressure groups. We have also filed a Public Records Access Request with the Board and hope that you're forthcoming with that information. Thank you.

Diane Lucas— I am Diane Lucas, President of the California Association of Teachers of English, an organization of 3,500 language arts teachers in California, and I would like to speak to the issue of process concerning questions about literature used on CLAS tests. First, there is, in fact, an existing process in place in the Department of Education by which any literature used on CLAS may be questioned. It seems to me that objections raised by any individual or special interest group about literature or literature response activities already approved for the CLAS test must follow this established procedure. The same protocol should apply to everyone: to parents, to students, to teachers, to special interest groups, or even to members of a California Board of Education. What's lacking here is integrity. The formal process already in place by which literature is questioned was carelessly ignored. Their removal is an insult to the expert California language arts teachers who have spent thousands of hours working on the CLAS Committee for the past several years. Yesterday sixty of my 10th and 11th graders read

Alice Walker's "Am I Blue?" What did they think the story was about? They thought, with no coaching from me, that the story was about people. Not one student mentioned the dietary preferences of the character. Even my least able student thought it was about differences between people. Other students mentioned ethnic diversity and that the story condemned racism. Those who claim the story promotes vegetarianism or feel the story discourages beef-eating either think more literally than my lowest-ability student, or base their challenge on some hidden agenda. They lack the very kind of critical or high-level thinking that the language arts framework and the CLAS test promote. If you want a generation that can only think on the most literal, superficial level, who will have little tolerance for the multicultural society in which we live, are easily manipulated by advertising slogans and by political groups, then present them with simplistic, white-washed, safe texts that could not possibly offend anyone nor any political agenda, right or left. This will be a society a totalitarian government would welcome, because they will be easily persuaded and easily controlled. Thank you.

Caroline Steinke— (This speaker has been yielded time by two other speakers. Although she does not mention it here, she is a representative of the Eagle Forum). First, for the Board members, I'd like to make available to you our assessment of the CLAS test, taken from depositions of children who actually took it. [McDowell, concerned about legal issues, delays handing it out.] First, I'd like to address the story of Alice Walker from the viewpoint of a student that took it. First of all, most students that would take the test would not know that the author was black, but if I were a mother who was black, I would be very, very upset at the portrait that was portrayed of a black mother who had five children without a husband, who'd given one away to a white man from Harvard. And I would be very upset that other children would be thinking that that is typical of a mother who during her wedding ceremony would be squeezing flowers and thinking of her children and choking. There are many things about these tests that I feel are very inappropriate. There is another story about a black boy, and if I were a black person I would be very upset that other people would be getting the impression that black families have fathers who don't care that children would rather go hungry than have their father home, or have mothers who are so insensitive to the needs of their children that they would send them out with a shopping list to go to the grocery store knowing that bullies could intervene and beat their children up. And when in fact it really happened in the story, and the child came back to his mother for comfort and affection, the child was given another list and told "don't come back, the door is locked, unless you bring the groceries". . . [Steinke is interrupted by McDowell, who asks her to "address the process not the content of the items."] This is not a censorship issue, this is a parents' rights violation, and I would like to read from the Federal Registry under "Students' Rights and Research: Experimental activities and testing." Mind you, the CLAS test is experimental. It has no research data to back it up. It's in process, and so this is very applicable. "For the purpose of this section, research, experimentation, program or project means: any program or project in an applicable program designed to explore and develop new and improved teaching methods and techniques. No student shall be required as any part of applicable program to submit to psychiatric examination, testing or treatment, or psychological examination, testing or treatment, in which the primary purpose is to reveal information concerning one or more of the following: number one, political issues; mental or psychological problems potentially embarrassing to student or his family; sex behavior or attitudes; incriminating, demeaning behavior; critical appraisals of another individual with whom the respondents have close family relationships; income, status of the family; without the prior written consent of the parents." These tests violate that; they violate Education Code 60650. We have many of the tests that violate these issues based on the prompt questions. Number one, here's one from . . . [Steinke is reminded by McDowell not "to discuss the items themselves" for security reasons.]

Okay, then let me address the assessment process and the scoring. First of all, these tests do violate the Ed codes, and we can prove it in a court of law, and we intend to do that, number one. Number two, we are asking the State Board to give us a response as to why, based on legislation, you have not produced by law what you are required to do. Number one, we are to have an individual assessment of our students on a yearly basis, and there have been none since the legislation was passed of SB662. Based on *individual* assessment. This year we had an assessment, but they were group scores, they were not an individual assessment, so we have been out of compliance with the law now since 1991. Also, in a press release on the 3rd . . . on the 9th, Acting Superintendent Dawson said that the CAP test is the old format and the CLAS test is the new format. We have both tests and they're both the same format. They ask the same types of questions. In other correspondence that we have, we have from someone from authentic assessment saying that they're really in fact the same test, just part of the process. Now let's talk about the California Learning Assessment Guidelines for Consortia Scoring. Number one, we parents are very concerned about what happens to these tests. Number one, when they come in, there is a copy made of them. It refers to specifically penciling them in, the copies, so that they are clear to read. I ask you what are you doing with the second copy of these tests. Under "Test Security and Student Confidentiality" I read: "Very early in the development of the CAP writing assessment [same process] teachers who were reading essays written in response to field test prompts discovered students were using the writing assessments to write about sensitive issues." I ask you, how does the School Board define a "sensitive issue"? If a person is in gender conflict, is his test flagged out? If a child is contemplating a sexual lifestyle, is his test . . . [Steinke is asked to conclude her thoughts because her six minutes are up.]

Basically, according to the scoring guides that . . . it is very difficult to come to basic conclusions on how these children score according to the double scoring. I ask you to look at it in the scoring manual, blind double-scoring and how after two scorers who do not match up the test a third one comes in, it doesn't match, then the scorers go back for recalibrating. I'm telling you this is a very difficult test to give a real honest to goodness assessment of our students to a standard.

Zita Rain— My name is Zita Rain; I'm an educator and school library media specialist. I welcome the opportunity to address the Board. California can be justly proud of its curricular leadership. It puts a premium on developing students who can think and respond with understanding based on real learning. Such students become the kind of educated, thinking citizenry which is so essential for a functioning democracy and a productive workplace. Now a new assessment system makes testing a part of students' learning, and provides further opportunity for students' informed response. Students who take the CLAS test have the opportunity we all wished for: to explain why they answer as they do, to provide a rationale that can be judged on the basis of their clarity of thought and ability to communicate, to read, and to understand. Literature—at the heart of the CLAS test— provokes thought and response. The test does not measure whether what the author says is right; it measures the students' ability to read with comprehension, to think, to react, and to communicate thoughts in writing. A student who reads literature with which he or she disagrees

85

may be moved to eloquence in disagreement. All students free to read and react are free to explore the basis of their own thoughts and feelings. There is no such thing as a non-controversial work of literature. There are always varying opinions about any work that is complex enough to be worth studying. How then can appropriate selections be made? Essential to all selection of materials is a process that establishes criteria based on curricular goals and student needs. The focus must be on the process for selection. This process begins with defining the curriculum and establishing curricular goals. Criteria for selection are based on these goals, and these criteria are established by those responsible for developing curriculum. In California, the development of the curriculum involved input from all segments of the professional and lay communities. Careful selection of materials is a thoughtful process in which evaluators, guided by common criteria, bring varying points of view and experience to their consideration of the work. Their choices reflect their judgment about how the selected work meets these published criteria. Withdrawing a work inherently involves withholding or restricting access to ideas or information. It is often perceived as an attempt to bring order to a confusing or challenging world. While demanding orderliness or conformity in thinking may seem comforting, easy to manage, less confusing, history demonstrates that it is always dangerous. Withdrawing a work or selection should never be based solely on mere objection of individuals, no matter how sincere or well-intended. It must be based on a process that allows for reconsideration that is as thoughtful as the original process for selection. Policies at state and local levels for the selection of materials also provide procedures for the challenge and reconsideration of materials. I believe that the recent actions of the State Board of Education and the California Department of Education, withdrawing three literature selections from the CLAS Language Arts Test, should be carefully reconsidered. My position is not based on my personal feelings, but rather on a reexamination of the process. I urge you to reexamine the process for selection and challenge of items on the CLAS test, that you withhold decisions about change until a clear process consistent with the objectives for the assessment instrument is established.

Joan Wandsley— I'm Joan Wandsley. I'm from the Southwest Riverside County Chapter of Eagle Forum. We're a pro-family organization; we're not a religious organization. I want to just address some of the concerns that parents have on the CLAS test. The issues that we have are not censorship but parent rights, violation of parental rights. Now a great deal of concern has arisen around the subject matter of the Language Arts Assessment. And the question that I have for parents is: Is this politically correct indoctrination, or is this assessing critical thinking? I think that's the key question here. In many districts the CLAS test is embedded into the curriculum, so although the CLAS tests are administered in April, they begin as early as September in preparing for the test. So what is it that has the parents and students that I have spoken with so appalled? It's the underlying themes of the stories that are used in the Language Arts Assessment. Here's what some of the students have said: that the stories tend to be racist, sexist, classist, anti-religious and anti-parent. Some of the stories touch on subjects such as environmentalism, gun control and the traditional institution of marriage. In more than a few stories, children are characterized as fatherless, alone and unwanted. The stories often reflect despair, death and hopelessness. Fathers are often stereotyped as abusive and insensitive. Some are uneducated, ignorant, gun-carrying clods. In not one of the stories that I've interviewed students on was there a positive role model of health. Not one. One student told me about a story that portrayed a teacher. There are two stories about teachers, one was Miss Marino at St. John's Catholic School, and she places a Hispanic boy . . . [At this point McDowell interrupts to ask Wandsley to talk about the process rather than specific test items. After some debate over the point, Wandsley proceeds.] The students that I have spoken with have talked about, and I am talking about . . . this crosses all racial barriers. I have talked to many diversity . . . much very different backgrounds, and what they have told me is that they feel that the role models that have been upheld in these stories are very negative, and particularly where Blacks or Hispanics are portrayed. [Timer rings.] They've been very negative . . . [McDowell asks speaker to conclude her thoughts.] One of the reports that I've read about CLAS test has said that the CLAS tests are designed to convey information to the reader. That's exactly what these CLAS tests are doing. And when I looked at all of the CLAS tests, those children are asked to persuasively write. They're supposed to be able to have a different point of view and come to a different conclusion after they've read these stories and be able to persuasively write about it. Now I just quickly wanted to tell you that I . . . [Wandsley is asked to conclude again, and is yielded additional time by another scheduled speaker.] Dr. Richard Paul, who is the director for the world-renown Center for Critical Thinking Institute at Pomona State University, says that the CLAS assessments routinely ignore critical reading and writing skills essential for students entering the job market, and Dr. Paul is highly critical of the California Department of Education for spending so much time and money on CLAS, which he calls "hopelessly subjective and ill-conceived." He calls CLAS a "colossal example of educational malpractice," and remarks that it "systematically rewards the wrong set of values, those which are subjective, idiosyncratic and irrational." What I want to say is that we are talking about parental rights here. We keep hearing about, "let the qualified educators do this work." I want to say that parents are qualified. Why are they qualified? Because they are taxpayers. They have every right to question curriculum. And they are systematically being told throughout this district that this is not their area.

Another thing I want to say is that parents are experts: they are experts on their own children. And they need to be able to have a voice about what kind of materials are put in front of their children, and they have been denied this right. Many of the parents I have spoken with have a very serious objection to the questions that ask for students' feelings and their thoughts and to relate their personal experiences. They feel this is invading family privacy, and indeed it is, and you're going to hear that over and over again, because that is what has been happening. And I've heard that from the students. And the students say these are weird and confusing tests. They have to write about thoughts and feelings. And they're based on erroneous, fictional accounts, so how can they come up with any objective conclusion or any objective answer based on the prompts that are used here? Thank you.

Gary Kreep— Good afternoon, my name is Gary Kreep. I've been an attorney for over eighteen years; since 1979 I've been Executive Director of United States Justice Foundation, a non-profit legal action organization. I've been active in education since 1983, and from July of 1991 to September of 1993 I served on the Human Relations Commission of the City of San Diego. I have had a chance to review a number of the CLAS tests and I must tell you that, if I had been sitting on the Human Relations Commission when I read two of these tests, and if they had been printed in a publication distributed at school, such as a school newspaper, our commission, I believe, would have taken action against that school district, because two of the ones, "Black Boy" and "Looking for a Job" . . . [Someone says "whoa," and McDowell asks Kreep not to refer to individual test items.] Well, first of all, under federal law, fair use doctrine allows me to mention those things because of the circumstances in which I am; I'm not reading any of the stories, number two; and number three, I didn't mention any of the authors, but those were from former CLAS tests, former, and I'd like to proceed. Thank you.

I've reviewed a large number of tests, and it is my opinion that, almost without exception, questions on these tests violate Education Code 60650 which prohibits any test, questionnaire, survey or examination containing any questions about the pupils' personal beliefs and practices, sex, family life, morality and religion, or same questions about the parents' or guardians' beliefs in those areas, without the parent or guardian first being notified in writing that the test was being given, and then giving permission. Now, in response to a request by an Assemblyman, Attorney Dan Lundgren in November issued an opinion saying that this section means what it says. It doesn't mean that tests involving these questions can only not be given if the parent objects. It says that school districts must affirmatively contact each parent and get their permission. Because of this, and because of my research of previous tests both CAP and CLAS, my organization sent a letter to the over one-thousand school districts in the state of California. We have advised them that if this year's CLAS test is the same as last year's CLAS test—and thereby violates Education Code 60650—and they give that test without obtaining written permission of the students, of the parents or guardian of the students to be given the test, we will initiate litigation against that district. Right now we have parents who have tentatively agreed to be plaintiffs in six counties and we will be initiating litigation. Part of the problem, of course, is that no one outside of this Board has apparently been allowed to see the 1994 CLAS test. So we don't know that the new test violates 60650. As part of the lawsuit we will be seeking a court order that they be reviewed by, judged by an independent committee to determine if they do. I should also mention that should we be forced to file these lawsuits, under the private Attorney [inaudible] we expect to see substantial attorney's fees awarded to the parents for being forced simply to protect their privacy and to enforce California law. Thank you.

Sue Thomas— Mrs. McDowell, members of the Board, I'm Sue Thomas. I teach English at Boron High School, and am a former member of the CAP writing development team, and I have been very active with literature projects and writing projects. Thank you for allowing me to speak. Before I resumed teaching high school in 1978, I spent seven years as a copy-writer for a large advertising agency in Sacramento. Once a week, or whenever we had a major new account, we had what we called a creative meeting. Before we came together, everyone involved was responsible for reading everything we could find on the subject of the meeting, and then for two or three hours, over many pots of coffee, we had a free for all discussion in which ideas—good, bad, and ridiculous—were accepted and noted, and gradually we began to see a plan emerge. At the end of the meeting each of us was assigned some piece of the work to draft and share. My piece was writing, writing enhanced by the ideas of a very diverse group of creative people with a common interest in the task we set ourselves. When I began to read about, and be involved with, the evolution of CLAS Language Arts Assessment, I was delighted to see it parallels how people work in the world, and that it reinforces that making sense of something is not necessarily about getting it right the first time or getting it right all by yourself. Humans are largely collaborative learners and that's part of the fun and excitement of learning. The CLAS assessment to me looks just like how we learn when we're doing it effectively. It asks students to read a story or an essay, mostly unfamiliar to them, and challenging to most or all, and then they're encouraged to do, as they read, what adult readers do in the workplace and in college: to mark up the text in order to make sense of it for themselves, to make connections to what they know, and to ask questions. At the end of the reading passage a variety of strategies allow them to think through what they read by writing about it, and then the second day allows them to discuss in the same kind of creative meeting that I had experienced, what they had read and make even more sense of it. Because of the diversity of my classroom, so much more comes out of that discussion than any individual student might be able to get. It's really amazing. It's also like what happens around the dinner table when the family problem-solves together. On the third day students show how they use what they understood by actually writing that understanding. When students make their understanding visible, teachers can teach more effectively, and this test, unlike multiple choice tests, makes this possible. Thank you.

Abby Barker— I am a member of the California Writing Project and Literature Project. I'm representing myself as a classroom teacher and a member of the CLAS Development Team. And I had planned to dazzle you with my credentials, but it seems that I have been impeached by several of the previous speakers in the allusions to the proper formation of families, of having a young woman to speak about what black families should be, how people should treat their children, whether or not people should have a father, and whether this . . . that is a value to them in determining what kind of person they are. And I have, I thought, a fine speech prepared, and I had to stop and reflect upon the bias that seems to be evident by several speakers in protection of, or defense of, your censorship. And I believe very strongly that it is censorship. And as a member of the CLAS Development Team, a member of the team that is comprised of educators, somebody referred to us as the "educational elite." I teach in Watts. That's my elite area. I have taught for thirty years. I and other members of the CLAS Language Arts Development Team which produced those prompts and recommended those stories that you took from us, got those stories, got those ideas, got those activities that have been deplored as attempts to invade privacy, got those from, if we put our experiences together, hundreds of years of teaching. We are not the elite. We are the people. We represent black, brown, Asian, Hispanic, purple, pink, different, the same, short, tall; we represent the children of this state, and I suggest to you that you follow your own policy, and that is clearly stated in the forward and the preface of the California Language Arts Framework, in which you state that your goal is to prepare our students to function in a democratic society, that you want to stem the tide of mediocrity, and to prepare our students to make decisions in this diverse society. We want the students to respect the differences, to celebrate the commonalities, and I don't think that your efforts are promoting that. I think that you are working in contradiction to your stated philosophy. I think that if the speakers who are urging that we purge this fine literature from our test—works that have for years worked with our students and in my classroom provided a lively forum for examination of ideas, for universal human concerns, for teaching us to be human and to be humane to each other—I suggest that had any of these people been students in our classrooms and experienced the activities, the literature, the discussion, the thinking, and yes, even the feeling, the challenging, the reflecting, the contradictions, the speculations, the critical examination of the human condition, I suggest that this hearing would not be necessary.

James Reed— Good morning ladies and gentlemen of the State Board of Education. My name is James Reed and I'm the outgoing Political Action Chair of the state NAACP, and I am a voice for African-American children in the State of California. As a former school board member, I too have made many tough decisions. But if there was room for error in that decision, I erred on the side of children. In your decision to remove the works of Alice Walker from various tests, you have committed a grievous error. That, not unlike other errors you have made, will again have a negative impact on African-American children. This Board and prior Boards have made decisions that have been guided by fringe groups such as the Traditional Values Coalition that tend to alienate students from diverse backgrounds, and have a direct impact on their self esteem, and consequently their ability to learn. When my children are not allowed to read works of authors that look like them, when my children aren't able to read of the achievements of people that look like them, when my children are prevented from reading stories of life experiences that are similar to theirs, then the travesty of this education continues, reinforced by the edicts of the State Board of Education. These children are using texts in their classrooms that say that Edison invented the light bulb, when Lewis Lattimer holds the patent on the filament, globe, and globe support, a bright lie that's being taught every day. When you as the Board of Education sanction selective censorship based along thinly veiled racial lines, you have stooped below those in Nazi Germany. When you cave into individuals who fail to respect the diversity of this great state, you give them official sanction to attack the hard-fought gains made by people of color over the years in this state. I ask you not to succumb to the temptation of taking the easy way out by granting those fringe groups their demands. And I ask you to be the guardians of education for children of all backgrounds. I appeal to you to reinstate this Pulitzer prize-winning author's work to the CLAS test. And I would like to just comment that it amazes me how many people have seen secured tests that have already testified in this audience. Thank you.

Sally Meyers— I've looked forward to being here today. I come to you with a little bit of a different perspective. I am not a teacher. I am a business person. I'm from Temecula and my field of study is in marketing, advertising and communications, and I've been in that field for about fifteen years. I also am an employer, and with that I come to speak to you today about my concerns. I'm an independent operator of Sizzler Restaurants in Southern California, employing about five hundred people. We have become increasingly aware of the students' lack of abilities in the basic education skills of reading, writing, math and other basic communication skills. A number of the students that work for us in our business, as well as in the rest of the hospitality and retail industry in their high school and college years, many of them determine, either possibly even with a college degree or after a college degree, they want to pursue management in our particular corporation. The reason that I come to you today is because in speaking with many of these students I have learned that many times they are told, or it is implied to them, that there may not be right or wrong answers in regards to the CLAS test and even with some of the studies that go prior to the CLAS test. And what I want to know is how that affects me as an employer when I need to have employees that are capable with math, grammar and reading and these types of skills. So as a business person I have kept up today with computer technology, marketing and advertising, advertising as it relates to my industry, and I believe that we do need to have computer literate students. However, we have power outages, we have equipment failures, and when this occurs, we need to rely on the basic skills, and that would be math, and we also need to know that our people can write orders, they can compute daily figures, and they can count back change, and even with this computer technology we need to make sure that our future employees have the use of basic weights and measuring skills, banking skills, etc., and that they can come prepared to us with those skills. Many of them are having a tough time today. I'm also opposed as a business operator to substituting basic educational skills for subjective-style learning assessment, which I have seen evident in the CLAS test, as in the Rosa Parks story, where students are asked to challenge or question authority. And if this is going to be the way of the future, it's going to be tough as an employer to be able to have students that have this type of philosophy. And also, as an employer, a taxpayer, a concerned parent—I'm a Board of Director in our Chamber of Commerce, a parent of three—I am opposed to the CLAS test as it is right now. And I'm opposed to having my children being able to reveal their personal values, beliefs and privacy as part of the test that I think should be more geared toward academics. I ask that . . . they say that the CLAS test does not instruct, measure or encourage competitive academics. We need that in the business world today. Please get back to the basics, and I do encourage you to allow students to opt out of CLAS.

Marty Kassman— My name is Marty Kassman. I'm an attorney from San Francisco. I speak today on behalf of Americans United for Separation of Church and State, which is a forty-seven year old non-profit organization dedicated to preserving religious liberty. Americans United has about fifteen thousand members nationwide, including several thousand in California, and I am Vice President of the San Francisco/Bay Area Chapter. Americans United has a perspective different from those of other organizations the Board is hearing from today. We're not here to support freedom of expression, although everyone I know in Americans United cherishes that freedom. Nor do we come to defend the literary value of the works that the Board ordered to be excluded from the 1994 CLAS exam. Our concern is with the apparent fact that religious objections were the basis, or at least one of the bases, of the decisions to remove Alice Walker's story "Roselily" from the CLAS exam and to remove an instruction that students express their feelings

96

about stories they've read on the test. I'll part from my written text briefly to note that in its lengthy presentation here today, the Department of Education staff did not offer any evidence, or even any representation, that there was any other reason for its actions. Public school officials have no business shaping the curriculum or testing to satisfy religious demands. By giving in to the Traditional Values Coalition, the state government has, in effect, given special rights to the advocates of one narrow religious perspective to the disadvantage of all those who subscribe to any other belief system. Now some people may be surprised at how much controversy these events have generated. It's important to understand that this episode is one skirmish in an ongoing nationwide struggle for the future of public education. For years Americans United and like-minded groups have engaged in battles all over the country against certain religious conservatives who seek to use the machinery of government, especially public schools, to impose their religious agenda on society at large. When religious right groups have gone to court to try to force public educators to remove materials that offend them, they have been unsuccessful. The courts have recognized, as the United States Supreme Court stated in 1968, that the state has no legitimate interest in protecting any or all religions from views distasteful to them. But there's no need for these groups to go to court if they can get what they want simply by demanding it from public education officials, as in the present case. Of course, the state must not interfere with the exercise of religious beliefs. For example, forcing a student to take a test on a day when his religion compels him to attend worship services would be inappropriate and unconstitutional. But it is equally inappropriate and unconstitutional to shape the content of a public school curriculum or test in order to satisfy religious concerns. What Americans United demands of this Board is simple: Make all of your decisions about the CLAS test and everything else based on what would make California's public schools as good as they can be. Thank you.

Beverly Sheldon— [Sheldon represents the Traditional Values Coalition, the organization that originally complained to the Department of Education about "Roselily."] Mrs. McDowell and members of the Board, the issue today is about process. What is the appropriate process for developing state tests? The California State Constitution has designated the California State Board of Education as the legal entity to oversee all education matters in California. In addition to this, legislation mandating these tests has repeated this constitutional oversight responsibility in Senate bill 662, passed in 1991. The State Board has instituted a legal process for the development of curriculum frameworks and textbook selections. Aside from what was presented [by the Department of Education earlier in the day], I do not believe such an extensive process exists, however, concerning this CLAS test. And that opportunity for community input is the only thing I am asking for: the same process the curricular materials go through before they are placed in the schools. Certainly some allowances need to be made so as not to compromise the integrity and privacy of the test. But a process that allows the opportunity for community input can be arranged, allowing for both broader input and privacy. We also need to be concerned because, as has been stated by your previous speaker, these tests are meant to be instructional as well as being tests. In the current situation, the educational elite are taking a false propriety. They don't think their choices should be under the same scrutiny as any...as every other educational document, even when they violate state education codes such as 60650. And according to these educationally elite, even the mandated State Board of Education and Department of Education cannot modify their work, the example being that the Board removed two of the documents, which they had every right to do without expecting rancor from the community. This is not a question of censorship, it's a question of process, because the tests our children take ought to be subjected to the same type of community input as their textbooks and curriculum framework. And I would also like to ask and bring to light...it appears to me that only two of the board members actually read these tests. And it seems to me that that needs to be modified, and if we have a problem of privacy, it would appear to me that maybe the legislature needs to mandate the fact that these tests can be looked at by the State Board in the same way that you look at legal things in a private matter. Because it seems to me the whole board should read these. Now also, as I look at the process that was given, I think that the Board needs to join the process at an earlier point [as it stands, the Board creates the frameworks and approves the final format of the test], possibly before it goes out for field testing and then again at the end. Thank you.

APPENDIX B:

The Color Purple Debates

Since its publication in 1984, Alice Walker's The Color
Purple *has been the site of considerable debate and controversy, primarily around two distinct sets of issues: first, the question of its suitability for younger readers, and second, the question of its portrayal of African-American men. (Concerns about the novel's portrayal of a lesbian relationship have figured strongly in both debates.) The following represents a brief outline of what has been at issue in these debates and some references for further information.*

*Language, Violence and Sexuality: Concerns
about Young Readers*

The occasion for most of the discussion about young people reading *The Color Purple* has generally been attempts by parents, school officials, or conservative organizations to remove the novel from library shelves and/or course reading lists. For a practical overview of the issues that usually arise in these debates, see Pepper Worthington, "Writing a Rationale for a Controversial Common Reading Book: Alice Walker's *The Color Purple*," *English Journal* (January 1985). The following is a partial listing of such incidents, along with a brief summary and references for further information.

Oakland, California— In May of 1984, a nearly year-long controversy started when Donna Green, whose daughter attended Far West High School in Oakland, complained to the Oakland school board about use of *The Color Purple* in district schools because she was "offended by the book's subject matter and graphic material." At the board meeting, Green handed out excerpts of the novel with "troubling" passages highlighted. In response to reading the passages, one school board member, Darlene Lawson, said: "I don't care if it did win the Pulitzer. As a black person, I am offended by this book, and we need to examine our policy on which books are allowed to be used." Green's daughter's classmates strongly opposed any attempt by an outside body to decide what they could read. "There was some bad language," said Susan Morgan, "but I felt the author put it there to be realistic, to show how the people talked. It's not there to excite anyone." The school board put together a committee of prominent local scholars and writers to review the novel. However, in early January of the following year, a measure to accept the committee's findings that the book was "entirely appropriate" failed to gain enough votes to pass. When the school board met the next week, it decided to approve of the use of *The Color Purple,* but to do so without mention of the committee's findings. (*Oakland Tribune,* May 3, 1984; May 4, 1984; May 8, 1984; June 22, 1984; January 11, 1985; January 17, 1985. *San Francisco Examiner,* May 5, 1984; June 22, 1984; January 11, 1985; January 17, 1985. *Newsletter on Intellectual Freedom,* July 1984, 103; September 1984, 156; March 1985, 42; May 1985, 91.)

Hayward, California— In March of 1985, as a direct result of student-led protest, school trustees in the Hayward school district met to review the book-buying procedure for school libraries. The meeting was the result of protests from students and faculty, claiming that the committee of school librarians, mandated by district policy to approve all book purchases, had acted as censors when they denied permission for the Sunset High School librarian to purchase *The Color Purple* and several other novels because of "rough language" and "explicit sex scenes." "We're not having books pulled off the shelf," said teacher Mary Walsh, "We're not getting the chance to put them on the shelf." (*Hayward Review,* March 19, 1985. *Newsletter on Intellectual Freedom,* May 1985, 75; July 1985, 111.)

Newport News, Virginia— In July of 1986, after flipping through a copy of *The Color Purple,* the principal of Ferguson High School, John W. Kilpatrick, decided that the book had too much profanity and too many sexual references. Although he had received no complaints from parents or students, Kilpatrick complained to the Ferguson media committee, which promptly decided to remove the book from the open shelves to be placed in a special section accessible only to students who are over eighteen or who have written permission from a parent. "I abhor censorship," Kilpatrick said, "At the same time, the materials in a public school library are there for a purpose." (*Norfolk Ledger Star,* July 15, 1986; August 4, 1986. *Hampton Roads Daily Press,* June 16, 1987. *Newsletter on Intellectual Freedom,* November 1986, 209; November 1987, 223.)

Saginaw, Michigan— *The Color Purple* was challenged at the Public Libraries of Saginaw, Michigan in 1989 because it was "too sexually graphic for a 12-year old." (*Newsletter on Intellectual Freedom,* May 1989, 77.)

Chattanooga, Tennessee— In July of 1989, a summer youth program came under fire from three parents (two of whom had not read the novel) for including *The Color Purple* in its curriculum. The program, which consists of half classroom instruction and half work experience, targets students identified as at risk for dropping out of high school. The parent who spearheaded the protest, Tricia Beeson, said, "The program is fine, but this garbage they're dishing out, I don't appreciate. It's just trash garbage to me." Another parent, state Rep. Bobby Wood, said that "any book that taxpayers buy should have some social redeeming values. I just feel like taxpayers in Chattanooga don't want to pay for children to read this kind of language." (*Chattanooga Times,* July 19, 1989. *Newsletter on Intellectual Freedom,* September 1989, 162.)

New Bern, North Carolina — In May of 1992, Patsy and Ray Gatlin, parents of a 10th grader complained about the use of *The Color Purple* as assigned reading. "If someone wants to read this book at home on their own, that's up to them," said Patsy Gatlin. "But when you take a child who has no choice and tell him he has to read it, that's different. Kenny's not going to read this book, not in school or anywhere else." In response to the Gatlins' complaint, an ad hoc committee reviewed the book and decided to allow Kenny to read a different book and modified the way the book will be taught to other students. The Gatlins' claim that they won't be satisfied until the book is no longer used in the system. (*New Bern Sun Journal*, May 7-8, 1992. *Newsletter on Intellectual Freedom*, September 1992, 142.)

Souderton, Pennsylvania — In 1992, the Souderton Area School District decided that *The Color Purple* was inappropriate reading for tenth-graders because it is "smut." (*Newsletter on Intellectual Freedom*, March 1993, 44; May 1993, 74.)

Junction City, Oregon — In early 1995, Chuck and Karen North launched a campaign to remove *The Color Purple* from the reading list for their son Ryan's high school English course. The Junction City chapter of the Parents for Academic Excellence took up the Norths' cause, mailing out to district families a page-and-a-quarter of "filth" containing every reference to the word "fuck" and each description of sex contained in the book, asking "Do you think this material lives up to Junction City's standards for academic excellence?" Also among their supporters was Henry Luvert, president of the local chapter of the NAACP: "I had to agree with him [North]. I felt like there was another agenda — a more feminist agenda at the expense of Black men." Nevertheless, at a school board meeting, school administrators and a majority of the community, including some religious leaders, supported *The*

Color Purple. Based upon recommendations by a book review committee, the School Superintendent decided that the novel could be used in the course's curriculum without restrictions, provided an alternative is offered. (*Eugene Weekly,* June 22, 1995. *Newsletter on Intellectual Freedom,* September 1995.)

Race, Gender and Sexuality: Concerns about Adult Readers

As Carl Dix suggests in "Thoughts on *The Color Purple,*" the attacks on Walker for what some have seen as her "negative portrayal of Black men" represented a continuation, and popularization, of an older controversy surrounding Ntozake Shange's *for colored girls who have considered suicide when the rainbow is enuff* and Michelle Wallace's *Black Macho and the Myth of the Superwoman* in the 1970s. The level of controversy has everything to do both with the fact that the novel was a best-seller and with its adaptation into a blockbuster film by Stephen Spielberg. Tony Brown provides perhaps the most succinct version of critics' objections in his article "Blacks Need to Love One Another": ". . . because so few films are produced with black themes, it becomes the only statement on black men. 'Purple' points us away from the fact that Nelson Mandela, Martin Luther King and Malcolm X overcame the system's pyschological warfare and produced healthy, non-incestuous, non-brutalizing relationships with women. Their women never needed a 'Shug.' Furthermore, most of us will be men in spite of white men and women who only publish books by black women or homosexual black men with degrading themes or passive attitudes—and then make them into movies of 'the Black experience.'"

Alice Walker's recent book *The Same River Twice: Honoring the Difficult* is probably the best single resource for examining various perspectives on her portrayal of African-American men. In it she not only responds to the criticisms but reprints several articles (including Dix's

104

and Brown's) representing varying positions on both novel and film as well as personal correspondence regarding the issue. The *New York Review of Books* published a particularly strong repudiation of both novel and film, in January of 1987: "Black Victims, Black Villains" by Darryl Pinckney. Another essay of interest is Richard Wesley's overview of the debate for *Ms.* (September, 1986): "If black women writers such as Gayl Jones, Audre Lorde, Ntozake Shange, or Alice Walker are to be hounded from one end of the country to another for decrying the insensitivity of black men to black women, then should not those black male writers such as Ishmael Reed be brought before some of these 'image tribunals' to account for *their* literary transgressions? But more important, there should be *no* 'tribunals' *at all*."

aunt lute books is a multicultural women's press that has been committed to publishing high quality, culturally diverse literature since 1982. In 1990, the Aunt Lute Foundation was formed as a non-profit corporation to publish and distribute books that reflect the complex truths of women's lives and the possibilities for personal and social change. We seek work that explores the specificities of the very different histories from which we come, and that examines the intersections between the borders we all inhabit.

Please write or phone if you would like us to send you a free catalogue of our other books or if you wish to be on our mailing list for future titles. You may buy books directly from us by phoning in a credit card order or mailing a check with the catalogue order form.

> Aunt Lute Books
> P.O. Box 410687
> San Francisco, CA 94141
> (415)826-1300

This book would not have been possible without the kind contributions of the *Aunt Lute Founding Friends:*

> Anonymous Donor
> Anonymous Donor
> Rusty Barcelo
> Marian Bremer
> Diane Goldstein
> Diana Harris
> Phoebe Robins Hunter
> Diane Mosbacher, M.D., Ph.D.
> William Preston, Jr.
> Elise Rymer Turner